Sick

by Zayd Dohrn

A SAMUEL FRENCH ACTING EDITION

FOUNDED 1830

SAMUELFRENCH.COM

MUSIC USE NOTE

Licensees are solely responsible for obtaining formal written permission from copyright owners to use copyrighted music in the performance of this play and are strongly cautioned to do so. If no such permission is obtained by the licensee, then the licensee must use only original music that the licensee owns and controls. Licensees are solely responsible and liable for all music clearances and shall indemnify the copyright owners of the play and their licensing agent, Samuel French, Inc., against any costs, expenses, losses and liabilities arising from the use of music by licensees.

IMPORTANT BILLING AND CREDIT REQUIREMENTS

All producers of *SICK must* give credit to the Author of the Play in all programs distributed in connection with performances of the Play, and in all instances in which the title of the Play appears for the purposes of advertising, publicizing or otherwise exploiting the Play and/or a production. The name of the Author *must* appear on a separate line on which no other name appears, immediately following the title and *must* appear in size of type not less than fifty percent of the size of the title type.

In addition the following credit *must* be given in all programs and publicity information distributed in association with this piece:

First produced under the auspices of the National New Play Network's Continued Life of New Plays Program at Kitchen Dog Theatre (May 2008), Southern Repertory Theater (March 2009) and New Jersey Repertory Company (February, 2009)

SICK premiered at Kitchen Dog Theatre in May, 2008 with the support of the National New Play Network's Continued Life of New Plays Fund. The performance was directed by Chris Carlos, with sets by Michael Sullivan, costumes by Christina Dickson, sound by Emily K. Young, and props by Judy Niven and Jen Gilson-Gilliam. The cast was as follows:

SIDNEY . . . . James Crawford

SARAH . . . . Martha Harms

MAXINE . . . . Lisa Hassler

DAVEY . . . . Lee Helms

JIM   . . . . Lee Trull

CHARACTERS

The Krebs family:

SIDNEY - 49

MAXINE - 46

SARAH - 19

DAVEY - 17

And a guest:

JIM - 26

SETTING

A Safe Haven on the Lower East Side of Manhattan.

For my parents

ACT I

(A house – immaculate, hermetically sealed.)

(Downstage is a sitting area: a couch, a chair, an ottoman, and a glass coffee table.)

(Two large air filter units stand in the corners of the room. They are towering, over six feet tall.)

(The windows are covered with shades, and the room is dark despite the daylight visible around their edges.)

(Downstage left is a foyer leading to the front door. Up left is a hallway leading to a bathroom and den. Up center, a door to the kitchen.)

(There is also a staircase up to the second floor.)

(In the half-light seeping around the shades, **MAXINE**, *46, comes down the stairs. She is dressed in simple cotton pajamas and a paper surgical mask covering her nose and mouth.)*

(She approaches the large air filter units and switches them on, releasing twin jets of vapor into the room.)

(The sound of boisterous laughter comes suddenly from offstage and **MAXINE** *jumps. She hesitates for a moment, listening, and then runs lightly into the kitchen.)*

(Just as she exits, the front door opens, and **SIDNEY**, *49, and* **JIM**, *26, enter, laughing.)*

(They are both dressed in sneakers and gym clothes, their shirts dark with sweat.)

(SIDNEY *wears a clunky knee brace, a headband, and glasses with a strap to hold them on his head.)*

(He carries two squash racquets and a small black duffel bag.)

SIDNEY. –Incredibly dirty. Filthy, I mean–

JIM. Can't wait.

SIDNEY. Oh, you'll love it, yeah. Disgusting. Right up your alley.

JIM. I'll take that as a compliment.

SIDNEY. You should. You should. The man was tragically out of place in the seventeenth century. Everybody else is out composing religious epigraph. Occasional poetry celebrating the birth of another inbred mutant, next in line to be Duke of Yorkshire or what have you, and this guy's out at court, seducing their wives with these smutty– take your shoes off, Jim, all right? *(tossing his own shoes on the floor)* –these smutty sonnets, satires. Absolute pornography. Of course, he did quite well for himself. You know, corseted aristocratic women love being talked dirty to…

*(**JIM** laughs, kneels to remove his sneakers.)*

JIM. You sound a bit jealous.

SIDNEY. Ah, well who wouldn't be? A libertine. A courtier, you know. Totally engaged in the world. *Living* his life. The precise opposite of the academic poet with his head in the clouds and his libido in a lock-box so as not to offend the fucking Pulitzer Committee. Of course, he caught syphilis. The just punishment for all godless perverts. His nose rotted right off his face, like a melting popsicle.

JIM. Lovely.

SIDNEY. He had to have a shnozz cast in bronze strapped to his head with a leather belt just to show his face in public. But he kept writing until his brain was liquefied. And screwing too, apparently. Dead at 33. It'll inspire you, I guarantee. Or at least turn you on.

JIM. At this point, either one would be fantastic.

SIDNEY. *(calling up the stairs)* Maxine? I'm home!

(no response)

Jim– Have a seat. I'll go get it.

JIM. Nice place.

SIDNEY. *(looks around)* Oh? Yeah, it's– I hardly notice, now, to tell you the truth... We bought it years ago, when things were cheap, so now we can't ever leave...

*(**JIM** laughs, and **SIDNEY** starts to exit.)*

*(**JIM** takes out an envelope, removes a type-written letter.)*

JIM. Sid, do you mind signing this now, or–

SIDNEY. Sure. Put it over there. I'll get my pen.

(He exits, towards the study.)

*(**JIM** puts down the letter, wanders over to one of the air filters and sticks his face in the jet of vapor, cooling off.)*

*(**MAXINE** enters, from the kitchen, still wearing her mask. She sees **JIM** and stops. He looks up, sees her through the clouds.)*

JIM. Hi– *(beat)* Jim... Sorry, one of Sidney's–

*(**SIDNEY** reenters, reading from a well-thumbed paperback.)*

SIDNEY. "Worst part of me, and henceforth hated most, Through all the town a common fucking-post, On whom each whore relieves her tingling cunt, as hogs–"

*(He sees **MAXINE** and stops. She hovers by the swinging door, motionless.)*

SIDNEY. Hey– Hon, I didn't hear– This is Maxine– come on in– my wife. Max, Jim.

JIM. Hello.

MAXINE. *(recovering herself)* Sorry, I was a bit. I didn't expect– Sidney, you didn't tell me you were bringing someone.

SIDNEY. Yeah, sorry. Spur of the moment thing. Kid was taking advantage of my advanced age over at the fitness center, and–

JIM. It was really close, actually.

SIDNEY. It was not. He mopped the court with me. And he's never even played squash before. Is that embarrassing?

JIM. I thought you were letting me win.

SIDNEY. I was, the first game.

(SIDNEY kisses MAXINE's cheek. She pushes him off.)

MAXINE. God, you're dripping with sweat, Sidney... You didn't even shower?

SIDNEY. No, there was a line. And we got to talking, and I realized Jim's never read the Earl of Rochester, which is a travesty, really, when you come to think about it. And we have two copies lying around here, just–

MAXINE. So does the bookstore.

SIDNEY. Yeah, well, Jim's a grad student, Honey. We can't expect him to pay for his own books. He needs that money for cigarettes, booze, and hookers.

JIM. True.

SIDNEY. Anyway, I wanted him to meet the family. It's a good subject for him, don't you think?

MAXINE. If you say so, Sidney... I just didn't realize I should have put down *newspaper* before you came home. *(She laughs. To JIM, confidingly:)* He's like a child sometimes, you know. Spends all day wallowing in the mud, and then comes home with his pockets stuffed with all sorts of... Would you like something to drink? I'm sure Sidney hasn't offered.

JIM. No, thank you. I should probably get home, actually.

MAXINE. Are you sure?

JIM. Yes, I've got a lot to–

MAXINE. Oh... Well then, it was really nice–

SIDNEY. No, wait. Stay. Have a drink, Jim. Keep us company. We insist, right?

(beat)

MAXINE. Sure. Bottled water? Juice? Wine?

JIM. Water would be great.

MAXINE. Ice?

JIM. No thanks.

(**MAXINE** *exits to the kitchen.*)

(**SIDNEY** *picks up the book.*)

SIDNEY. *(reading)* "–On whom each whore relieves her tingling cunt, As hogs do rub themselves on gates and grunt."

(**JIM** *laughs.*)

JIM. I can see why we didn't cover him in eleventh grade English. Mrs. Crenshaw would have had a stroke.

SIDNEY. It's a shame though, don't you think? High school boys are the ideal audience for this stuff... *(tossing* **JIM** *the book)* Here, bone up.

JIM. Thanks.

SIDNEY. I got to play the Earl once, you know, at an MLA colloquium. A bunch of us dressed up as writers from history: Milton, Blake, Shelley, Langston Hughes. We're supposed to be having this serious conversation about– "genre" something or other. And I'm sitting at the table, with my bronze nose, powdered wig, and massive leather codpiece. Shouting about my "clammy joys" and "liquid raptures." Surprised it didn't end in a lawsuit, actually. Some terrified librarian...

(**MAXINE** *reenters, with a glass of water only a tiny bit full.*)

MAXINE. Here you go.

JIM. Thanks. Great.

(*He puts the book down on the coffee table and takes a careful sip of water.*)

MAXINE. So, you're one of Sidney's students? A poet?

JIM. Trying to be.

MAXINE. You must be good. He only likes the good ones.

(**JIM** *smiles, embarrassed.*)

JIM. I haven't written anything good in years, to be honest.

SIDNEY. He's being modest. He's very talented. Although, he did drop a full letter grade at the gym today.

JIM. Sore loser.

*(**SIDNEY** laughs, drops his duffel bag on the couch. **MAXINE** goes around to the chair and notices something on the carpet.)*

MAXINE. Oh, Sidney, look! You tracked *mud* all over the floor!

SIDNEY. What mud?

MAXINE. Look, it's–

SIDNEY. We took our shoes off as / we came in.

MAXINE. Well, is this mud, or / isn't it?

SIDNEY. Honey, there's no way–

(She kneels, sniffs the carpet.)

MAXINE. Uh! It's not mud.

SIDNEY. No?

MAXINE. No! It stinks, Sidney! It's dog shit. God, look at that.

SIDNEY. Look at our shoes, Maxine. They're in the foyer. Safe and / contained.

MAXINE. It's on your *socks* then. How does anyone get shit on his socks? Do you just walk around barefoot all day looking for filth to stomp through with your disgusting meaty hooves?

*(**JIM** nervously checks his socks.)*

SIDNEY. Our socks are clean, Max. Look. Maybe somebody tracked it into the locker room at the gym then, and it's on… I don't know. I'm sorry, all right?

(beat)

*(**MAXINE** laughs. She pulls her surgical mask down so it hangs loosely around her neck.)*

MAXINE. *(to **JIM**, lightly)* It should be illegal, don't you think, Jim? In Singapore they just shoot all the dogs. To keep the city clean. Here we put them on leashes, wander around, and let them *spray* the sidewalks. And then we clomp through the manure like we're living on a farm, and nobody seems to notice. Nobody cares. In a few more years, people won't even be able to walk. We'll all need skis and snowshoes to get around... You're not a dog lover, are you?

JIM. Not especially.

MAXINE. Good. Suddenly I thought I might have put my foot in my mouth. I do that sometimes. Luckily, I don't track through *feces* first, like Sidney does.

JIM. Ha. I prefer cats.

MAXINE. Uch! Cats, blechh. You don't have cats at home, do you?

JIM. Uh... Well, my parents have two, but–

MAXINE. No, but you don't live with them now?

JIM. My parents? No. I'm a little bit / old for–

MAXINE. I meant the cats.

SIDNEY. Leave it alone, Maxine. You're embarrassing him.

MAXINE. Am I?

JIM. No, that's all right.

MAXINE. He seems quite confident.

SIDNEY. Don't let the good looks fool you. He's shy.

   (beat)

MAXINE. Sidney had a rat once, you know, when we met–

JIM. Really?

SIDNEY. A hamster, actually.

MAXINE. A rodent, anyhow. He kept it in the kitchen, can you believe that? Next to the sink. Every time we had breakfast, I just wanted to barf. Finally, I dumped the squeaky thing down the garbage disposal and hit the switch. *(She imitates the sound.)* I'm joking, of course.

JIM. Ha...

SIDNEY. Hilarious.

MAXINE. We gave it away. The pound or something, wasn't it, Sidney? Do they have a pound for hamsters?

SIDNEY. All right, Maxine. Enough.

MAXINE. Enough what? This is called "small talk." I'm entertaining our guest. Somebody has to. You can just walk in and throw crap on the floor, but when I try to–

SIDNEY. You've made your point... I'll clean it up.

MAXINE. No, don't bother. Don't bother. You'll just smear it around and make it worse. *(to* **JIM***)* Have you ever noticed that men are incapable of cleaning up the slightest mess? I think it's because you pee standing up, you never really practice a proper wiping motion. Every day I mop an absolute carpet of pubic hair off the bathroom floor. The boys don't even seem to notice.

(**JIM** *laughs, politely.* **MAXINE** *puts her mask back on and exits, to the kitchen.)*

SIDNEY. Sorry about that... We have kind of a cleanliness fetish going on here. In case you hadn't noticed.

JIM. It's all right. My mom's a neat freak, too.

SIDNEY. A "neat freak." Well, that's a good way of / putting it.

JIM. I didn't think we– tracked anything in here though, honestly.

SIDNEY. No. She– imagines things, that's– I'm afraid Max has kind of um...lost track of what's real and what's... *(He trails off.)*

JIM. Whatever the opposite of real is?

SIDNEY. Hm. Exactly. *(He smiles.)* In any case, you're here now. An outside observer. A witness to our surprise.

JIM. What surprise?

SIDNEY. Oh, well. We could all use a bit of objectivity, Jim. What do they call it? In a science experiment? The "control?" I'm an inmate here myself. Can't very well study the asylum, now can I?

JIM. Well, you both seem like you're on the spectrum of normal to me.

(**SIDNEY** *laughs.)*

SIDNEY. Wait a while.

(**MAXINE** *enters, carrying a bucket and a rag.*)

JIM. You've got a great place here, Maxine.

MAXINE. Thank you. We bought it when things were cheap, so now we can't ever leave.

SIDNEY. I already told that one, Honey.

(*She laughs, pulls the mask down again.*)

MAXINE. Oh, well... Married couples are so tedious, aren't they, Jim? It's like sharing one brain. One small, feeble, bisected brain.

(*She starts to clean the carpet.*)

JIM. Can I–

MAXINE. That's all right. I got it... Are you from the city?

JIM. No, from Michigan, actually.

MAXINE. Oh, whereabouts?

SIDNEY. A hick from the sticks, Darling. We'll have to instruct him on the mysteries of sidewalks and / traffic lights.

JIM. Just outside of Detroit, actually. Thank you very much.

MAXINE. (*pleasantly*) I love the Midwest. I'm from Milwaukee, originally. It's so much more wholesome, don't you think? Compared to the coasts...

SIDNEY. "Wholesome." Ugh.

MAXINE. Really. You know that since 9/11, New York City has been the most polluted place on the planet, Jim?

JIM. I didn't, no.

MAXINE. Yeah. The EPA did an environmental assessment, they won't even release some of their findings. There'd be mass exodus. If people knew– We're blanketed in clouds of asbestos, vaporized plastics, VOCs, lead paint, jet fuel. It's all carcinogenic. Not to mention the consequences for sufferers of asthma and allergies. It's like we all just inhaled two office buildings. In our lungs. Three hundred fifty stories of steel and concrete and glass, along with three thousand bodies.

Charred flesh, human hair, bone. Cut ten years off the life expectancy of every person in the city, probably. And we're worried about global warming? *(She laughs.)* Of course, Sidney won't even think about leaving Manhattan. He's like Woody Allen. Except not funny.

(**SIDNEY** *laughs.*)

JIM. My friends all thought I was nuts to move here now. They all think it's a matter of time, you know, before the next biological attack, or dirty bomb...

MAXINE. Well they're right, but actually that's the least of our worries now. Look at the *air*. I mean, we're living on top of this giant *cesspool*. And then we're surprised by these massive upticks in premature births, infant asthma, lung cancer, autism?

SIDNEY. *(interrupting)* How are the kids, Maxine?

MAXINE. Oh, they're– *(She glances at the stairs.)* Sarah's running a slight fever, I think, but she's pre-menstrual, so maybe that's normal, I'm not sure. Davey hasn't had a bowel movement since Tuesday... I've given him a laxative, but–

SIDNEY. So, they're fine.

MAXINE. Well, if you don't want *details*, Sidney.

SIDNEY. You kidding? I love details. Tell us more, please**...** Let's break out the spreadsheets.

MAXINE. *(to* **JIM***)* I'm sorry. Our children are *ill*, so–

SIDNEY. That's a matter of opinion.

MAXINE. Is it?

SIDNEY. Why don't we call them down? Introduce Jim to the next generation.

MAXINE. They're studying.

SIDNEY. They can take a break. Anyway, how's he supposed to form an accurate opinion if he doesn't get the full freakshow?

(beat)

MAXINE. All right, fine... Call them down. If you want to take that risk.

SIDNEY. That *risk?* That's a bit dramatic, don't you think? I mean our guest will start to feel unwelcome here. He's not some disease– Some spore we might accidentally inhale.

JIM. I'm sorry, maybe I should–

SIDNEY. *(without turning)* Sit.

MAXINE. *(laughs)* Don't worry, Jim. Stay. Relax. It's fine. A familiar squabble. It comes out of affection. Mostly. *(to* **SIDNEY***)* Well then… At least clear your things off the couch, Sidney. This isn't a toxic waste dump, after all.

(She picks up his duffel bag.)

MAXINE. What's this, your dirty jock strap?

SIDNEY. Yes, Max. It's so big I need a separate *bag* to carry it around in.

(For some reason, both **SIDNEY** *and* **MAXINE** *find this very funny. They laugh.)*

*(***MAXINE** *drops the bag on the coffee table as* **SIDNEY** *goes to the foot of the stairs.)*

SIDNEY. *(calling)* Sarah? Davey? Come down a minute?

(He crosses back to the sitting area. **MAXINE** *puts her mask back on.)*

MAXINE. *(re: the dog shit)* Don't mention this to the children, Jim, all right? They'll worry themselves sick. Who knows what this *mutt* had in his system. The fleas. Worms–

*(***SARAH***, 19, and* **DAVEY***, 17, appear at the top of the stairs. They are pale, fragile, kind of weirdly beautiful.)*

*(***DAVEY** *has on a paper mask like* **MAXINE***'s, covering his mouth and nose.* **SARAH***'s face is uncovered.)*

*(***JIM** *stands as they come in.)*

JIM. Hello–

SIDNEY. Guys, this is Jim. One of my students. Sarah. Davey. Our kids.

JIM. Good to meet you.

SIDNEY. Come. Chat.

> *(They come down the stairs together and sit on the couch, across from* **JIM**.*)*

> *(***JIM*** sits too, uncomfortably aware of his own body, his damp clothes.)*

JIM. Sorry… We just came from playing– I'm a little bit–

SIDNEY. Jim's in my class this year, guys. I thought he and Sarah might be able to talk shop.

SARAH. James– Corrigan? Is that your–

JIM. Uh, yeah, how did you..?

SIDNEY. Sarah reads all the literary journals. *Kenyon Review. Threepenny.* Cover to cover, right? Keeps track of the new talent.

JIM. Oh.

SIDNEY. She knows an up-and-comer / when she sees one.

JIM. I don't know if I can still / be considered–

SARAH. I don't keep track. You make me sound like such a stalker. *(to* **JIM***)* I hate most of it. Just love to torture myself with mediocrity, that's all.

JIM. Thanks.

SARAH. Oh, I don't mean you. I didn't mean– I like some of yours… The early ones. "Inside-Out Man." That was good.

> *(beat)*

SIDNEY. Davey? Are you gonna say hi?

DAVEY. Hello.

SIDNEY. Jim's the best writer in the program this year. A future star. Although his grade did drop a full letter on the court this after–

MAXINE. You already used that one, Sidney.

SIDNEY. So I did. I did… *(He chuckles.)* Jim, you want to stay for dinner? You must be starving.

> *(***SARAH*** and **DAVEY** both glance at **MAXINE**. She watches **SIDNEY**.)*

JIM. Oh, I don't think I can, I'm uh–

SIDNEY. Come on. We don't get visitors often. Keep us company. We'll call it extra credit.

MAXINE. Sidney, I don't have enough for–

SIDNEY. We'll supplement. Must have something lying around. Leftovers? Ten minutes. Jim, what do you say?

JIM. I'm not really dressed.

SIDNEY. It's not black tie.

JIM. Well, but I don't want to intrude...

SIDNEY. Oh, come on, mealy-mouthed Dear Abby social etiquette bullshit! You're a starving poetry student. Your professor just invited you to a free dinner. Complimentary calories. Eat!

JIM. *(laughs)* Okay.

SIDNEY. All right then. I should warn you though, we have vegans here, so if you want a T-bone or foie gras, look elsewhere.

JIM. No, I'm pretty much a vegetarian myself, actually.

MAXINE. Are you?

SIDNEY. Well then, you'll fit right in. The only animals we like to slaughter in this house are dogs and– what? Hamsters, Max?

(**SIDNEY** *laughs.*)

(**DAVEY** *suddenly takes a deep, rattling breath.*)

(*They all look at him.*)

SARAH. Davey?

SIDNEY. Hey, what / is it?

MAXINE. You having a reaction?

(**DAVEY** *nods*)

SIDNEY. *(to* JIM*)* No problem. Don't worry–

MAXINE. What is it, Honey? Can you tell? Something on the–

SIDNEY. Why don't you go upstairs, Dave. Rest a bit.

MAXINE. We'll turn on the filters. Clear it out. Okay?

(**DAVEY** *nods and makes his way carefully up the stairs, holding the railing.*)

JIM. Sid, I should really go– You guys have a lot going on here, and I'm–

SIDNEY. Don't be ridiculous. This happens sometimes. Asthma. He just needs to lie down, take some deep breaths. He'll be okay. Trust me, he soldiers through. You'll get used to it. I still have to sign that letter, right? After dinner.

(**DAVEY** *has disappeared upstairs. The others sit in an awkward silence.*)

SIDNEY. Maxine? Shall we?

MAXINE. Are you trying to make a point, Sidney?

SIDNEY. What point would that be? It's not as if this is unusual, is it? You don't think it's anything *serious?*

(*beat*)

MAXINE. Sarah? Are you–

SARAH. I'm fine, Mom.

MAXINE. You sure?

SARAH. Yes.

SIDNEY. We'll let them talk then, okay? (*to* **JIM**) You washed your hands, right? You're sterile?

JIM. As a mule.

(**SIDNEY** *laughs.*)

SIDNEY. Smart ass. Believe this kid? (*ushering* **MAXINE** *into the kitchen*) Ask her about her work, Jim. Don't take no for an answer. Trust me, she *wants* to talk about it.

(**SIDNEY** *and* **MAXINE** *exit.* **JIM** *and* **SARAH** *sit there, awkwardly.*)

JIM. So. Your work..?

SARAH. Guess you're Dad's new favorite, huh?

JIM. Uh. I wouldn't say that. Just a / student.

SARAH. "Friend?"

JIM. I don't know. I guess we hit it off. A bit.

(She nods at the piece of paper on the coffee table.)

SARAH. Recommendation letter?

JIM. Yeah.

SARAH. Made you write it yourself, didn't he?

JIM. *(laughs)* I did a draft, yeah. He's a busy guy, so– I don't mind.

SARAH. I hope you were lavish in your praise. You mind?

(She picks up the letter.)

JIM. Uh– It's a little embarrassing, actually. I'd prefer if you didn't–

SARAH. *(reads)* "James Corrigan is the most talented and promising young poet I have met in over two decades of teaching–" Wow. Congratulations.

JIM. He told me to be "obscenely generous," so…

SARAH. What's it for?

JIM. A fellowship. At Stanford. I don't know…

SARAH. Just what we need, right? More Stegner poets. Gag.

*(**JIM** laughs.)*

He took you to play squash though. That's a good sign. He must think you're good. He chooses someone each year, you know. We hear all about that. He believes in um… Apprenticeship. One-on-one guidance. The ancient Greeks. Of course, he's never brought one of you home before…

JIM. I'm honored.

SARAH. Are you?

JIM. Shouldn't I be?

SARAH. I think it's annoying, actually, picking favorites based on this macho male bonding bullshit. Squash? *(She picks up the book.)* The Earl of Rochester? How's a woman supposed to get noticed if the professors all prefer men?

JIM. *Many* of the professors notice women, trust me.

SARAH. Gross.

JIM. *(laughs)* Well… Better that he hangs out with me then?
At least we know his intentions are pure.

SARAH. He took me to play once, you know, when I was a
kid. I was scared. Whacking a ball around a room the
size of a refrigerator, it seems insane. And the locker
rooms there are *filthy*. Like trekking through a sewer.

JIM. Imagine what the guys' room is like. Ten times worse.
At least. *(beat)* Hey– Your dad said you wanted to talk
about your work, right? Can we–

SARAH. No, I don't–

JIM. "Don't take no for an answer."

SARAH. Too bad.

JIM. Uh… *(laughs)* Okay… I can't force you.

SARAH. He's just trying to be provocative. Ignore him.

JIM. Tell me something at least, so I can say I–

SARAH. "Tried?" What do you want to know?

JIM. Something about– something you wrote? Anything?
I'm interested, really…

SARAH. Yeah, right…

JIM. No, I am. I am. Come on.

(**SARAH** *looks at him.*)

(*She reaches in her pocket and takes out a folded piece of
paper. She unfolds it and glances at the page.*)

(*She rubs the piece of paper between her fingers, considers, and then holds it out to him.*)

(**JIM** *takes the paper. He reads, looks up at her, reads
more. She watches him carefully.*)

(*He puts the paper down.*)

JIM. Guess it runs in the family, huh?

SARAH. Oh please.

JIM. I'm serious. I'm not even surprised. I mean, your dad's
a genius, after all. Maybe it's hereditary.

SARAH. Genius genes, you think?

JIM. I'm jealous. How'd you come up with this? If you don't mind my–

SARAH. Oh, I saw a documentary once. Discovery Channel. About a group of spiders, in Africa? They had gotten so big they could hunt live chickens–

(**JIM** *laughs.*)

And there was a picture of this one spider, standing over a dead bird. This big. *(She demonstrates.)* He had dragged it out of a coop in the village, like a coyote. And when they took the cameras down into the spider hole, where all these huge things lived, feeding on KFC, they found a live frog down there, with all the spiders… They were keeping it, as a pet, bringing it food, and cleaning up its waste, grooming it–

JIM. *(laughs)* That's the sickest thing I ever heard.

SARAH. I know, isn't it? I felt so bad for the frog though. Don't you think? Down there, all alone, with those things? This foreign species? But I don't know, maybe he was happy. Maybe they were friends. Maybe he felt taken care of… *(beat)* So, I wrote a poem about it.

JIM. Sent it out yet?

(**SARAH** *shakes her head.*)

Why not?

SARAH. I don't know. Uncomfortable.

JIM. Your dad knows people. He could probably–

SARAH. Oh, yeah, No, I know. I just don't want to have people shitting all over my poems right now. They're private.

JIM. You showed me.

SARAH. I was curious.

JIM. About what?

SARAH. Whether they're any good.

JIM. You must know they are.

SARAH. I wanted– an outside opinion.

JIM. Why me?

SARAH. Because you're here. Because you're a guy. Because
    I'm pathetic and insecure. I don't know. I was trying
    it out.

JIM. And?

(*SARAH shrugs.*)

(*He looks at her.*)

Hey– Can I ask you something?

SARAH. What?

JIM. How old are you?

SARAH. Why..? Nineteen.

JIM. I knew it.

SARAH. What?

JIM. Child prodigies *depress* me. A reminder that I'm old
    and fucking *ordinary*. I'm twenty-six, right? When I was
    nineteen I was probably writing like– white-boy rap
    lyrics and dirty rhymes on the bathroom stalls.

SARAH. I'm not a child.

JIM. You're still in high school?

SARAH. No, I've graduated, basically.

JIM. "Basically?"

SARAH. Well, we're home-schooled, you know... Mom's a
    certified high school teacher. I have a diploma. But
    there's no ceremony or anything. We had a cake. They
    bought me a laptop.

JIM. You made out like a bandit, trust me. Ceremony's the
    worst part.

SARAH. Yeah...

JIM. So you're applying to colleges now, or...

(*beat*)

SARAH. Keep a secret?

JIM. I think so. Sure.

SARAH. I already applied. To St. John's? In Annapolis? I was
    accepted. Got the package yesterday.

JIM. Congratulations.

SARAH. Yeah. They have excellent health services there, you know. One of the best in the country. Ten full-time doctors, and an ICU right on campus–

JIM. Wow.

(She blushes, realizing she's said something strange.)

SARAH. I have a family history, you know, so I have to think about–

JIM. No, sure. I understand. I'm just–

SARAH. Going away to college would be–

JIM. A big step.

SARAH. Right. *(beat)* My mom doesn't know yet. That I applied. That I got in. We didn't want to upset her, until. So. It's gonna be a big surprise tonight.

JIM. I'm sure she'll be ecstatic.

(She nods uncertainly.)

So what did you mean "the early ones"?

SARAH. What?

JIM. You said before. You liked my "early ones…"

SARAH. Oh, I don't know. I just–

JIM. You think my recent stuff is–

SARAH. No no no, I–

JIM. Shit, right? *(He laughs.)* That's why I came to New York. Hoping for…inspiration. Or something. That your dad would rub off on me.

SARAH. And has he?

JIM. Not yet. Not yet, but I'm hopeful. Another year before I have to throw in the towel, go to law school or something…

(beat)

SARAH. Hey, you want to hear some music?

JIM. Sure, what do you–

SARAH. Bach? Shubert..?

JIM. Oh, fine. I'm illiterate with that kind of– I know more like, The Ramones. The Cure, y'know…

SARAH. Punk music.

JIM. Well… Nerd-punk by now, I guess.

(She nods awkwardly, gets up, turns on the stereo. Music starts to play.)

*(**JIM** mock-cheers, making the sound of a crowd at a rock concert. It falls flat.)*

*(**SARAH** sits back down.)*

JIM. So… You don't wear a mask.

SARAH. No.

JIM. Your mom said you were sick.

SARAH. Mmm. My brother's mostly– Well, we're all allergic to certain things. Borderline MCS? So. We have to keep the place clean. Immaculate, really. It's kind of a full-time job, for all of us. But as long as I'm here, I'm pretty– safe.

JIM. You must be able to see germs just leaping off me.

SARAH. Oh, I don't think so. You look very clean.

JIM. Well, if I'd known, I would have showered, at least.

SARAH. *(laughs)* Anyway, I'm not as sensitive as he is. I can handle it. You.

(They both try to think of something else to say.)

JIM. So, there must be places to go to get help for this kind of–

SARAH. Oh, there are. Sure. Support groups. "Detox Centers."

JIM. And?

SARAH. I don't know. I go on their websites, and they're all– *(a new-agey voice)* "Welcome…to the place…of non-toxic…healing…" Pastel colors, you know? Little animated birdies tweeting in the corner of the page. So cheesy, I can't bring myself to call. I worry, you know, sometimes, that I make all the choices in my life that way.

JIM. What?

SARAH. Aesthetically? Like I have no moral or rational core, just– Taste.

JIM. Taste can be moral. If you're into balance, right? Proportion? That's all justice is, really– I guess. I think… *(beat)* So you know, there's a reading tonight, on campus. Graduate student poets, if you're interested… Open mic. Check out some of the competition… If you want, you could read your work, make us all look like amateurs.

*(During this conversation, **DAVEY** has come onto the landing at the top of the stairs, toting an oxygen tank on wheels and a removable plastic mask.)*

(He stands there quietly, breathing through his mask and listening.)

SARAH. Why? Are you reading something?

JIM. Might be. Get a couple drinks in me. You never know.

SARAH. I haven't– done anything like that in a while… Ever, actually.

JIM. So, it'll do you good. Get some fresh air. Hear some bad rhymes. Drink a beer or two. Couldn't hurt, right?

SARAH. No, I don't think–

JIM. Or you could just listen. No pressure.

SARAH. Maybe some other time.

JIM. You think your dad would mind? My asking..?

SARAH. No no, he– he'd like it. Probably be thrilled if I left the house once in a while… Drank a beer. Ha.

*(At the top of the stairs, **DAVEY** removes his plastic mask and takes a loud, rasping breath.)*

*(**SARAH** jumps up from the couch, turns off the music.)*

SARAH. Hey– Davey..?

DAVEY. Sorry. Filter's broken.

SARAH. Oh. *(She goes to the bottom of the stairs.)* Want me to take a look?

DAVEY. Could you? Sorry. My eyes are all blurry. I can't really–

SARAH. No problem. Come on.

(*She starts up the stairs.* DAVEY *hesitates.*)

DAVEY. I'll sit with Jim, okay? Keep him company... Is that all / right with you?

SARAH. You sure? You feel up to it?

DAVEY. Yeah. I'm okay. Just needed to catch my breath.

(DAVEY *makes his way over to the couch, dragging his oxygen tank.* JIM *jumps up to help.*)

DAVEY. I got it. It's okay.

JIM. You sure?

(SARAH *helps* DAVEY *sit.*)

SARAH. You all right?

DAVEY. Yeah.

(*She hesitates, hovering over him. She glances at* JIM.)

SARAH. You know, Davey's really good at magic–

JIM. Oh yeah?

SARAH. You should get him to show you a trick.

JIM. Absolutely. That'd be great. I love magic.

DAVEY. Are you a magician?

JIM. No. No, I'm a good audience though. I never know how anything works.

DAVEY. You have a quarter?

(JIM *fishes in his pockets, takes out a quarter.* SARAH *takes it, wipes it, and hands it to* DAVEY.)

(DAVEY *raps it twice, loudly, on the table, and shows his hands. The coin has disappeared.*)

JIM. Wow... I'm impressed.

SARAH. (*laughs*) But you lost a quarter.

JIM. I guess I did.

(DAVEY *touches* SARAH*'s mouth and produces the quarter.*)

Damn.

SARAH. Amazing, isn't it?

JIM. Yeah.

DAVEY. It's really easy, actually.

JIM. I know I couldn't do it.

DAVEY. I could teach you. Simple.

JIM. Yeah… That'd be great, Dave. Sometime…

(beat)

SARAH. So, you sure you guys are okay?

(**DAVEY** *nods.*)

Okay… I'll be back in one minute.

(**SARAH** *glances at* **JIM** *and then runs up the stairs and exits to the second floor.*)

(**DAVEY** *takes several long hits from his oxygen mask. He takes the mask away.*)

DAVEY. Sorry about that… I get these, sometimes.

JIM. No / problem, are you–

DAVEY. *(overlapping)* I wanted to get a chance to– *(beat)* Sorry. What were you gonna say?

JIM. Nah, go ahead.

DAVEY. You.

JIM. Oh. Okay. I was just– uh. I was going to ask if there's anything I can do, Dave, if you're–

DAVEY. No, it's no problem.

JIM. You sure?

DAVEY. I was hoping we could have a little guy talk, actually. Man-to-man?

JIM. Yeah, of course. What do you want to–

(**DAVEY** *takes a hit from his mask.*)

DAVEY. You must think this is all pretty weird, huh?

JIM. No, I don't. I think it's–

DAVEY. I would, if I were you. You're healthy. You walk around. You breathe the air. It must seem so fucked that people can live like this, in a bubble…

JIM. I don't feel that way. People are different.

DAVEY. The way I see it, there's two possibilities… Either
we're defective, y'know, mutations, and natural
selection is busy getting rid of us as we speak… Or
we're the canaries in the coal mine, and the rest of
you fuckers are next. *(He laughs.)* I was tested once,
you know, when I was a kid. Okay. Out of 99 house-
hold chemicals, I was allergic to 94. Bleach, ammonia,
preservatives, food coloring, whatever… That's pretty
much off the charts.

JIM. Wow.

DAVEY. Yeah. I had serious reactions to sixty-eight of
them… My mom only scored a thirteen, by comparison. So. It's because of me she stays inside. Because I
can't leave.

JIM. That must be hard, Dave. Lonely… I'm sorry.

DAVEY. Well, I have my family. Some people don't even
have that.

JIM. That's true.

   *(**DAVEY** takes another hit from his mask.)*

DAVEY. Hey– Can I ask a question?

JIM. Sure. Of course.

DAVEY. You must have had a lot of experiences… Outside.

JIM. Not compared to some. I'm kind of a homebody,
actually. Spend most of my time in my apartment,
staring at the computer screen–

DAVEY. I mean, with girls.

JIM. Oh… With girls? Well, not really, "a lot," then, I
wouldn't say–

DAVEY. But you've had some?

JIM. Some…experiences?

DAVEY. Yeah.

JIM. You mean–

DAVEY. Like–

JIM. Have I..?

DAVEY. Forget it.

JIM. No. No, I just– I wasn't sure what you meant, Dave. You mean…sexual–

(**DAVEY** *just looks at him.* **JIM** *laughs awkwardly.*)

I'm sorry. That's not what you meant? I didn't mean to–

DAVEY. No, it's fine… If you *want* to talk about it.

JIM. Okay. Um… What did you / have in–

DAVEY. Does it feel the way it looks?

JIM. "The way it looks?"

DAVEY. In videos.

JIM. Oh. Uh-huh. Okay…

DAVEY. I've seen some. Online.

JIM. Right. Gotcha.

DAVEY. So, I know what it looks like. But I've never actually–

JIM. Right. So you want to know, is that what it feels like.

DAVEY. Yeah.

JIM. Um. So, can you describe the way it looks to you? Just so I–

DAVEY. Sweaty.

JIM. *(laughs)* Well, those people are under the movie lights, Davey, you know. So it's probably pretty warm. But I guess it can be sweaty…

(**DAVEY** *nods, absorbing this.*)

DAVEY. It looks like it hurts.

JIM. Well, that could be the acting, maybe…

DAVEY. I have one clip of a man with two penises. Do you think that's real?

(**JIM** *is overwhelmed. He laughs.*)

JIM. I have no idea, Davey. I'm sorry, you got me there. I kind of doubt it.

DAVEY. He's got one right here, and another one right here. He can do two girls at one time, or one girl in both holes.

JIM. Sounds uncomfortable.

DAVEY. It's pretty amazing, actually.

JIM. I'll bet.

DAVEY. Maybe in the future everybody'll have two. You know? You'll have to, in order to attract a partner, so it'll become evolutionarily advantageous, and eventually indispensable.

JIM. A whole race of mutant porn-stars, yeah. Love it.

DAVEY. Of course, I'll already be extinct by then... Women are loaded with my worst reactors: perfume, nail polish, hairspray, tooth bleach, nylon stockings...

JIM. Wow.

DAVEY. So I'll never be able to have kids, probably. *(He takes a hit from his mask.)* My sister doesn't use that stuff, because she's allergic too. She doesn't use make-up or anything. She's pretty, though, anyways, don't you think?

JIM. Yeah, she is.

DAVEY. She looks like my mom, when she was younger. You should see pictures... Spooky. Nothing like my dad at all.

JIM. You two must be pretty close, huh?

DAVEY. For sure. We're like twins, practically, being together all the time... We never really had a peer group with whom we could socialize, so– We make friends, you know, online. But it's not the same.

JIM. No.

(beat)

DAVEY. So. Are you interested?

JIM. What?

DAVEY. In my sister?

JIM. Oh, no. I mean– I think she's *interesting*... Is that what you–

(He glances at the staircase.)

DAVEY. It's okay. I put a piece of a Q-tip in the filter. It'll take her a while to figure it out... We can talk, guy-to-guy.

(beat)

JIM. I'm not sure you should have done that, Davey.

DAVEY. It's okay. I do it all the time. She practically expects it, now. She spends a lot of her time, you know, taking care of me, so–

JIM. Why?

DAVEY. Because. I need her.

JIM. But I mean– Don't you take care of each other? I thought she was– y'know, *like* you in that–

DAVEY. No, she's sensitive, but nothing like me, Jim. Nobody's like me... I'm like an astronaut away from his home planet. If I didn't have my space suit, I'd just be blown away...

*(**SIDNEY** enters, from the kitchen, wearing an apron.)*

SIDNEY. Almost ready, Jim. You guys getting along..? *(He sees **DAVEY**.)* Hey– Where's Sarah?

DAVEY. Filter's broken. She's fixing it.

*(**MAXINE** enters, wiping her hands with a dishcloth.)*

MAXINE. Feeling better now, honey?

DAVEY. Yeah. We were just talking.

JIM. Can I help, Sid? With dinner, or–

SIDNEY. Everything's ready. Let's get her down here...

MAXINE. I'll go.

SIDNEY. No, I got it. Stay.

*(He goes up the stairs to find **SARAH**. **MAXINE** sits down with **JIM** and **DAVEY**. There is an awkward pause.)*

JIM. Smells good...

MAXINE. I can't take credit. I'm hopeless, in the kitchen, Jim. You live in New York too long, certain parts of your brain start to atrophy. What are you two chatting about?

DAVEY. Guy stuff.

MAXINE. Oh? Should I leave?

JIM. No!

DAVEY. We're done. He was quite informative.

MAXINE. Good, I'm glad. *(to* JIM*)* It's difficult, you know, for one person, to teach them everything they need to know. Especially their mother.

DAVEY. We had a sex-ed unit, as part of our curriculum last year. You should have seen her, trying to put a condom on a cucumber.

(He laughs. MAXINE *smiles.)*

MAXINE. I embarrassed myself, I'm afraid.

DAVEY. No, it was interesting.

JIM. You're not allergic, Davey? To– latex, or–

DAVEY. Oh, yes. We used Naturalamb.

MAXINE. Always an awkward conversation, with your children… Your parents ever talk to you about "the birds and the bees" Jim?

JIM. Yes. In a moment of pure existential horror for all of us.

DAVEY. You should read *The What's Happening To My Body Book For Boys.* It's excellent.

JIM. Huh. I'll check it out, Dave. Thanks–

*(*SARAH *and* SIDNEY *appear at the top of the stairs.)*

SIDNEY. Hey. Everybody? Listen up. Before we eat, Sarah has a little announcement to make.

(He comes down the stairs, leaving SARAH *alone on the landing. They all look up at her. She glances around nervously.)*

SARAH. Now..?

SIDNEY. No time like the present, huh? "The Moving Finger writes; and, having writ / Moves on…"

SARAH. Uh… I didn't think it was / going to be–

MAXINE. Sidney..?

SIDNEY. Come on. It's exciting news. Out with it. Don't be shy.

*(*SARAH *turns and goes into one of the rooms upstairs.)*

(**MAXINE** *glances at* **SIDNEY**, *but he avoids looking at her.*)

(**SARAH** *reappears after a few seconds, holding a glossy college admission packet. She holds it in front of her like a shield.*)

SARAH. Mom– Davey. Surprise! I got into college... St. John's. Start in September... Full scholarship. They want me to come for an orientation in July. "Students with non-traditional educational experiences," so we can all meet and get acclimated to the classroom environment. Look– personal letter from the Dean.

(**MAXINE** *looks around, bewildered.*)

MAXINE. When did this happen?

SARAH. Yesterday. We found out. I wanted to tell you all day, but–

MAXINE. How did you–

SARAH. We worked on it last summer. Collecting forms, and writing essays. It took a long time, really. But we wanted it to be perfect before–

(**MAXINE** *looks at* **SIDNEY**.)

MAXINE. We?

SIDNEY. Congratulate her, Maxine.

MAXINE. *(looks around)* Well, tell me details.

(**SARAH** *comes down the stairs, in a rush.*)

SARAH. It's a small school, Mom. Only five hundred students. I think you'll like it. Really. Excellent English Department. Dad knows some of the professors there. By reputation. And ten percent of Freshmen were home schooled, as kids. So they appreciate the independence of thought and experience that comes from–

(**SARAH** *has approached* **MAXINE**, *holding the packet out like a gift.*)

(*When she gets close,* **MAXINE** *slaps the envelope out of her hands.*)

MAXINE. Don't! Bring that close to your brother, Sarah! It's reeking of photo fixer! I can smell it from here.

(Beat.)

(They all stare at the envelope.)

(SARAH kneels and starts to pick up the scattered papers.)

(JIM comes to help.)

SARAH. I'm sorry... I didn't–

MAXINE. Plastic. Colored ink. Stamp adhesive? What's gotten into you, Sarah? Really, I mean–

JIM. Here, I got it.

SIDNEY. Max–

MAXINE. It's out of the question, Sidney. A dorm room? A cafeteria? She wouldn't last a week.

SIDNEY. She's an adult. She can make that / decision for–

MAXINE. It's too dangerous.

SIDNEY. There are doctors there. It's not the third world. I mean, her reactions are completely under control lately. They haven't been *serious* / anyway in as long as I can–

MAXINE. It's dangerous in other ways! She's inexperienced. She doesn't know how to / protect herself.

SIDNEY. She'll learn.

MAXINE. You know what could happen...

SIDNEY. No, I don't know. Nobody knows what could happen, Max. It's unpredictable. It's called living / in the world.

MAXINE. They could hurt her...

(SIDNEY makes a sound in his throat, slightly hysterical.)

SIDNEY. Who? Photo chemicals? Plastics?

SARAH. Dad, don't–

MAXINE. You've seen what can happen.

SIDNEY. Who are we afraid of here?

SARAH. Dad, forget it... I won't go. Please don't fight–

SIDNEY. Look at you, Maxine. The three of you. Huddled inside this place like there's been some nuclear holocaust! And every day, I come home to this bunker, and you look at me like I'm this piece of shit that just defiled your sacred space! Like I'm carrying some *contagion* in my skin!

MAXINE. You are! You track things in from out there! You're not careful... I've tried to tell you– To explain, but–

SIDNEY. Things from out there? I bring home *food*, Max... Medication... Without me, this manufactured cocoon would disintegrate in a week! I *enable* this insect existence! Well, no more. You want to eat, you go outside. You want replacement filters, go to the fucking hardware store!

MAXINE. You want to kill us, go ahead!

SIDNEY. Nobody's killing anybody! Here. Look–

(He goes to the cabinet, opens the door.)

Bug spray... I brought it home last week...

(He opens another cabinet, rifles through the contents, pulling bottles from the back, dumping them on the floor.)

Cheez Whiz!

(another cabinet)

Engine oil... Wiper fluid... Rat poison... Air freshener!

(He takes out an aerosol can and sprays it into the air.)

SIDNEY. It's been here for weeks. The whole apartment. The city. The stores. Everything, inside... And nobody even noticed! Look–

(He picks up his gym bag, which has been sitting on the coffee table. He unzips it, tears open a plastic bag, and dumps it.)

(Hundreds of little white pellets scatter on the table and roll across the floor.)

SIDNEY. *(cont.)* Mothballs, Max! Volatile Organic Compounds... Sitting here since I got home– Emitting! Right in front of us. And nobody got sick... Nobody died. Look at it, Maxine! It's you! It's not real! The whole fucking thing was just– in your head...

(long pause)

(SIDNEY stands there, panting, holding the empty gym bag.)

(Everybody is quiet.)

(MAXINE is perfectly still, frozen.)

(SARAH looks around.)

SARAH. Davey..?

(Everyone glances over at DAVEY.)

(He looks back at them, confused.)

(His plastic oxygen mask is slowly filling with blood.)

(Curious, he reaches up and removes the mask.)

(Blood pours out of his nose and mouth, spilling all over the floor.)

SIDNEY. Oh...

(DAVEY sinks to his knees, staring at the blood on the carpet.)

(His eyes roll back in his head, and he collapses on his back.)

SIDNEY. God.

MAXINE. Shit– Sarah! Get the kit–

(SARAH runs into the kitchen as MAXINE drops on her knees next to DAVEY, who has started to shake, his fists clenched.)

JIM. I'll call 9-1-1–

MAXINE. No! No ambulance! They'll make it worse– Sarah!

(SARAH runs back in with a medical kit, and MAXINE expertly inserts a tube down DAVEY's throat.

(**SIDNEY** *has backed up against the wall, watching.*)

(**DAVEY** *starts to convulse violently, and* **MAXINE** *wraps her arms around him, trying to keep him still.*)

(*She turns to* **SARAH**.)

MAXINE. Get it, Sarah. Quick! Flush him out! Flush him–
   (*blackout*)

END OF ACT I

ACT II

(A little while later.)

*(**DAVEY** and **MAXINE** are gone.)*

(The floor is littered with mothballs swimming in a small puddle of blood, engine oil, and Cheez Whiz.)

(The windows are all open, the shades pulled up to air out the room, the filters turned off.)

(Outside, it is dark. The sounds of traffic. The city.)

*(**SIDNEY**, **SARAH**, and **JIM** are on their hands and knees, cleaning up.)*

SARAH. You really got the full treatment tonight, Jesus...

JIM. Mmm.

SARAH. Did he tell you about the man with two penises?

*(**JIM** laughs, shakily.)*

SIDNEY. Guys– Don't make fun.

SARAH. No. We're just–

SIDNEY. He's a– really good kid, actually.

JIM. I know he is. Sorry.

SIDNEY. You can go if you want, Jim. You don't have to be–

JIM. I'd like to stay. Until we hear how he's doing, at least? Otherwise I'm up all night, worrying... Unless I'm in the way..?

SIDNEY. No.

*(**JIM** nods. They work silently, picking up the wet mothballs one by one.)*

*(Finally, **MAXINE** comes down the stairs.)*

(Her smock is stained, and she looks haggard, exhausted. She still wears her paper mask, slightly askew.)

(SIDNEY staggers to his feet as she enters.)

SIDNEY. Hey– Max…

(She ignores him, pushing past him and into the kitchen.)

(SIDNEY looks to SARAH and JIM, but they avoid eye contact, absorbed in their cleaning.)

(He stands there, adrift.)

(After a few moments, MAXINE returns, carrying a Brita filter and a paper towel.)

SIDNEY. Max, please… How is..?

(She pushes past him again.)

He's all right? Tell me. Please. Is he–

(She goes up the stairs.)

(SIDNEY stands there.)

SIDNEY. Guys… I'm sorry. Jesus. I didn't know– Honestly… *(beat)* Sarah..?

SARAH. I'm okay, Dad.

(He nods, looks around.)

SIDNEY. Can *allergies* do that? Make you react like–

SARAH. He gets nosebleeds, sometimes. Thin nasal membranes. They / rupture easily.

SIDNEY. Is that what that was? A nosebleed?

SARAH. I'm sure he'll be okay.

(SIDNEY nods. Beat.)

SIDNEY. Jim, what a horrible… I'm so– embarrassed.

JIM. Please. I'm fine. The last thing I want is for you to worry about me…

(SARAH unfolds a cotton bag and JIM dumps some of the wet towels into it.)

SIDNEY. I was going through our files, last month... I found our wedding pictures, sitting in an envelope. Probably in there since we moved. Those old prints are full of photo fixer. That's supposed to be one of Davey's worst reactors. So I got rid of them. Scanned them at work, and then threw the prints away. I didn't say anything. Didn't want to cause a scene... But that got me thinking. He's around those files all the time. Why didn't anything happen? Why no reaction? So last week, when we had those water bugs in the bathtub, I brought home a roach motel, full of– roach poison? Or whatever? Stashed it behind the toilet. I watched, to see if anything happened. Nothing. For three more days. And no roaches either. I started– picking out other things, from the grocery store. Bleach. Oven cleaner. I got more and more excited, with every piece I brought home. Felt like I was– curing him, some-how...

SARAH. We got this, Dad. Why don't you go upstairs?

(SIDNEY *has been picking up mothballs with a white towel. He stops.*)

SIDNEY. You go, honey. I'm sure he'd like to– You shouldn't be down here anyway.

SARAH. Don't you start.

SIDNEY. I'll take over here. See Jim off.

SARAH. I can help. I'm fine.

(MAXINE *has appeared on the stairs.*)

MAXINE. He's right, Sarah. You shouldn't be exposed.

SARAH. Mom, is he..?

MAXINE. Come on. Up you go. Bedtime.

SARAH. I'm fine. Is Davey..?

MAXINE. He– went into shock. His fever spiked to a hundred and four, for a second, which was... Well. He bit off a piece of his tongue.

(SIDNEY *covers his eyes.*)

MAXINE. But he's not hurt. Permanently– There's no sign of nerve damage. I think he'll recover, if we're careful...

SIDNEY. His tongue..? Max–

MAXINE. There's not much blood, once it's all cleaned up. It was a little piece.

SIDNEY. Can I see him?

MAXINE. No, I don't think so, now. He's resting.

SIDNEY. Maxine, please–

MAXINE. I don't want to upset him, Sidney.

SIDNEY. I won't. I won't talk, or– I just want to look at him.

MAXINE. What for?

SIDNEY. I'm– Because I'm concerned.

MAXINE. *(matter-of-fact)* You tried to kill him.

> (JIM *stands up, starts to go.* SARAH *grabs his arm, holds onto him.)*

SIDNEY. No! No, I– thought I could help him. I thought. I was doing you all a favor. To open your eyes–

MAXINE. It worked, Sidney. They're wide open now...

SARAH. Mom.

MAXINE. I never saw anything so cold. So viciously calculating in my entire–

SIDNEY. It was a mistake– I thought I was–

MAXINE. What? Winning the argument?

SIDNEY. No. Doing something– Just to– Break the inertia... To do *something*, I thought–

MAXINE. Congratulations, Sidney. You have acted. Definitively. We are all in awe of your masculine *agency*.

SIDNEY. ...

MAXINE. You brought that poison in... Planned it, for weeks? Like an assassination attempt. Lee Harvey Oswald. *(She picks up a can of Cheez Whiz.)* Look. The murder weapon. *(She laughs.)* It'd be comical, if it weren't so completely–

SIDNEY. It was a mistake. I didn't see.

MAXINE. Oh, I know.

SIDNEY. I was trying to help.

MAXINE. Sure. *(beat)* Why do you stay with us, Sidney? That's what I can't understand. Anymore. You hate us so much...

SIDNEY. I don't hate you, Honey– Christ, I was trying to *save* you.

(She starts up the stairs again. He grabs her arm.)

MAXINE. Get off–

SIDNEY. Max, listen–

MAXINE. Let me go.

SIDNEY. You were right, okay? I didn't realize. How toxic the outside could be, for Davey– I'll admit, I thought it was– So much of what goes on in this house is just– difficult for me to understand... I thought, when he didn't react all week, it was definitive. That he was–

MAXINE. Reactions can be delayed. I've told you that.

SIDNEY. Yes... I know, but–

MAXINE. It was probably outgassing the entire time. All those chemicals, building up in his system... Multiplying his load... And then you shoved it in his face like that, all at once, Sidney. Of course he reacted. He could have *died.*

(She pulls away, continues up the stairs.)

SIDNEY. *(desperately)* Here, look– Look at me, Max. Please–

(He takes a paper mask from the first-aid kit and puts it on, covering his nose and mouth.)

(He goes to the bottom of the stairs, showing his covered face, like an offering.)

(She looks down at him.)

(long pause)

MAXINE. We'll have to clean this up, you know.

SIDNEY. Of course.

MAXINE. Wipe the room. He can't come downstairs until we've gotten rid of every piece– Every trace. If he steps on something– *smells* something, even… He'll be especially sensitized, now. You should close the windows.

SIDNEY. You're right. We'll clean. Go. Sarah and I can handle–

(He starts to shut the windows.)

MAXINE. You'll have to shower too. Change your clothes. Clean your hair and nails, if you want to see him now…

*(**SIDNEY** looks up at her.)*

SIDNEY. Now..?

MAXINE. He asked for you… If you're ready.

*(**SIDNEY** nods.)*

*(He touches **MAXINE**'s hand, and she moves out of the way, letting him past.)*

(He makes his way up the stairs and exits.)

(long pause)

*(**MAXINE** starts to follow him, and then hesitates, halfway up the staircase.)*

MAXINE. Jim. I'm sorry you had to be here for–

JIM. No. Don't worry.

MAXINE. I appreciate your trying to help. Honestly.

JIM. Please, it's nothing.

MAXINE. We must seem so rude… Are you hungry now?

SARAH. Ha.

JIM. No, I'm– Thanks. I'm okay.

MAXINE. You sure? We never had dinner. You must be… I have a pathological Jewish mother nightmare that people will starve to death in my house.

JIM. I'm fine, really.

MAXINE. *(She smiles.)* We're not always like this, you know. We can be very…normal. And fun. On good days. But

maybe it is better after all that you understand why–
That you see what we're up against here. That it's no
laughing matter. That there are things we can't risk,
with… *(She glances up the stairs.)* If Sidney had told
me he invited someone, I would have tried to– To
make arrangements. I don't want you to think we're
ungracious, or that we didn't like meeting you, but
obviously there are people who are very sick in this
house. We're not really set up for visitors.

JIM. I hope Davey's okay.

(beat)

MAXINE. Sarah? You really should go upstairs until the
room is cleared. I know you don't feel it yet, but–

SARAH. I'm okay, Mom… I'll just say goodbye to Jim, finish
the cleaning, all right? I feel fine… I want to do something.

*(**MAXINE** nods.)*

MAXINE. Don't stay too long, okay? Your reaction could be
delayed too. Better safe than sorry.

SARAH. Yeah.

*(**MAXINE** exits, upstairs.)*

*(**SARAH** starts to clean up a puddle of Davey's blood
with a wet rag.)*

(long pause)

JIM. You okay?

*(**SARAH** nods.)*

JIM. Wow. That was quite a–

SARAH. Yeah. It was.

JIM. I think I might be having a delayed *heart attack*.

*(**SARAH** laughs.)*

SARAH. I can't believe you're still here. You're very intrepid.

JIM. No, I've had worse. I went to dinner with a friend of
my mom's once, and she talked to me all night about
gardening. Yecch.

(She smiles.)

SARAH. Well, I think you've fulfilled your good Samaritan duties for the *year* by now. If you need someone to sign your letter, I'll do it.

(JIM picks up the letter, which is soggy with blood and chemicals. He shows it to her, and then drops it in the bag.)

JIM. Can I ask you something?

SARAH. Yeah, of course.

JIM. Has anything like that ever happened before? I mean, is it always like that, when he–

SARAH. "Like that?" Well, let me see… On his birthday once, we accidentally gave Davey a set of treated wax candles. He foamed at the mouth and collapsed on the cake. Burned off one of his eyebrows. And when they sprayed dad's department with insecticide, he came home without changing clothes, and three of Davey's molars fell out. So– "Like that." I don't know…

JIM. Nightmare.

SARAH. Mmm.

JIM. And it's all *real*, do you think, or–

SARAH. What do you mean, "real?"

JIM. I don't know… I mean, in his head, maybe? Sid seemed to think it was– psychosomatic, partly, or–

SARAH. What's the difference? It happens.

(beat)

JIM. Well, what about you?

SARAH. What about me what? *(beat)* Oh, I'm not so dramatic. *(She laughs.)* My symptoms are really tame by comparison. Boring, actually.

JIM. Can you tell me about them? Or, is it private..?

SARAH. No, I– guess not. I just get these little *petit mal* seizures, sometimes. Everything gets very flat, like a pop-up-book. My senses get squeezed, like I'm being folded up inside. And I pass out. It's scary. But it only lasts a second.

JIM. So you could probably deal with that. If you wanted to. I mean, with help?

SARAH. Yeah. Easy for you to say.

(beat)

JIM. Sorry. I just meant, it's not life-threatening… Like it is for Davey? You don't have to stay / inside, your whole life.

SARAH. Really? Are we playing doctor now?

JIM. I don't mean to–

SARAH. You're outside, Jim. You can't understand. I mean, look at what / happened just now.

JIM. Okay. You're right.

SARAH. It's not your fault. You just. Can't.

(They are silent for a while, cleaning.)

JIM. So, what about college?

SARAH. What about it?

JIM. You're still going? St. John's?

SARAH. Ha. That idea didn't go over too well, in case you hadn't noticed.

JIM. Look, I know it's not my place, all right, but–

SARAH. You're right, it's not.

JIM. But still– I feel like I should say something. You're too talented / to waste your–

SARAH. I know what you're gonna say, all right? Don't. It's not so simple.

JIM. It can be. You're nineteen.

SARAH. And what? Old enough to run away?

JIM. Maybe.

SARAH. Get a job? An apartment? I mean– look at me…

JIM. I could help.

(She shakes her head.)

SARAH. I can always go later, if things get… Maybe it's for the best, anyway. At least here I can work, you know. I can write.

JIM. You can write at school. At a coffee shop. A bar. You don't have to be locked in the house all the time to–

SARAH. Maybe I do. Who knows?

JIM. That's ridiculous.

SARAH. Is it?

JIM. Yes. I'm sorry, but– That's not how genius works, Sarah. It doesn't come from being a crazy lady in the attic. A / cloistered nutcase–

SARAH. Oh, and how would you know how genius works?

(She exits.)

(beat)

(JIM *stands there for a moment.)*

*(***SARAH** *comes back in.)*

SARAH. Sorry. I'm sorry…

JIM. No, it's okay.

SARAH. I didn't mean–

JIM. No. You're right. You're absolutely right.

SARAH. No no. Honestly, that's not what I meant. I wasn't thinking. I'm a total bitch.

JIM. Please. By the time Keats was my age, he was dead. I'm not blind. I do have a shred of self-perspective. *(He chuckles.)* You know, when I was little, I used to have this fantasy… I'd pretend my dad hit me… Abused me, somehow. I'd lie awake at night, imagining I had black eyes, busted lips, blood in my mouth, that kind of thing… I was nine. Ten. And he was– the last guy in the world who would hurt– a cockroach, even, let alone his own– But. I thought, to be a great artist, you had to be tortured, right? Come from some twisted, freakish upbringing. And my parents were nothing if not normal. So I'd do things to him, trying to provoke a reaction. I'd be like "Dad, I have a secret to tell you" and I'd hock up a lougy in his ear. Tear the covers off his books, that sort of thing… And he'd look at me, when I did those things, hurt and confused. And I'd feel like a complete asshole. But I kept doing it. I couldn't stop. Even later. A teenager. I wanted him to suffer for being so fucking *nice*. You know? For making me *ordinary*. And one day I told him: "I hate you. You're pedestrian. Nothing about you is fascinating to me at all. You're not even a person!" And he hit me. Finally. Right across the face. Little back-handed karate chop. I was completely stunned. Too shocked to feel it, even. And we both stood there, quietly. And then *he* started to cry...

SARAH. You should write a poem about it.

JIM. I did... I thought you–

SARAH. Oh. Is that– what that one was about..?

JIM. Forget it. *(beat)*

SARAH. So, what's your point? I'm lucky? My freakish family– Is that the moral? You want to fucking *trade*?

JIM. No, I'm just saying... I'm saying, you don't have to make yourself miserable, Sarah... Live in a cave, like–

SARAH. I'm not miserable.

JIM. You should go to school. Publish. Join the world. Be in conversation, with other artists, and–

SARAH. Emily Dickinson never published.

JIM. Emily Dickinson was a sad virgin shut-in who never left the house!

SARAH. Well, so am I!

JIM. What? Sad? Shut-in? Virgin?

(beat)

SARAH. None of your business.

JIM. I'm sorry. I thought you were–

SARAH. What, propositioning you?

JIM. Confiding.

SARAH. I'm not. I'm not, I barely know you... You're a complete stranger to me, and I– I think you should go now.

JIM. Really?

SARAH. Yes. Now. Please?

    (beat)

    (He stands.)

JIM. I'm sorry. I'm an idiot.

SARAH. It's okay.

JIM. No, I am.

SARAH. It's fine, Jim.

JIM. You're not gonna deny it or anything? Just to be polite? No?

    (Pause. They stand there.)

    Okay. I'm gonna go then...

    (He starts to leave, glances back at her, hesitates, looks closely at her face.)

SARAH. What?

JIM. Sarah..?

SARAH. Yeah?

JIM. I'm sorry. I don't mean to be– Your face is just getting kind of–

SARAH. What's wrong?

JIM. Some kind of rash. On your cheeks– Look–

    (She touches her face self-consciously.)

SARAH. Don't– do that.

JIM. Shit. I'll go get somebody.

SARAH. No, just–

JIM. Your mom.

    (He starts up the stairs.)

SARAH. Wait, Jim– Hold on.

JIM. What if it's– delayed? It could be serious. We should at least check with–

SARAH. I'm *blushing*, okay? *(beat)* I do that, sometimes. Sensitive skin. It's not a "reaction." Fuck. I'm *embarrassed*, that's all.

    (beat)

(He comes back down the stairs, approaches her.)

JIM. Look– We'll make a deal, okay? Come out with me tonight. Hear some drunk idiots do an open mic. Have a beer. Get some life experience. If it doesn't totally inspire you, I'll admit you were right, lock myself in my closet, and stare at the wall until I write *Paradise Lost,* okay?

SARAH. That could take a while.

JIM. Two, three hundred years, tops. I work really fast.

(She smiles.)

SARAH. And does having a "life experience" include going to bed with you?

(beat)

JIM. We'll leave that part optional. But– If you want to be a miserable tortured poet though, you should at least get to be a *debaucherous* miserable tortured poet. Look at Byron. Whitman. Jorie Graham...

SARAH. *(laughs)* You're kind of a cad, I think.

JIM. A "cad"? Really?

SARAH. Not that I have much to compare it to, but... Do all normal guys talk like this?

JIM. Only the desperate ones. *(beat)* Come on, is it a deal or what? Don't make me beg. I feel pathetic enough already.

(She hesitates.)

SARAH. I'm blushing again... Yeah?

JIM. A little bit.

SARAH. Skin. Always betrays me... So annoying.

JIM. Know what you mean... Fucking skin–

(He reaches for her face.)

Pimples. Rashes. Scars. *Really* annoying...

(He touches her cheek. She flinches away, but he keeps his hand there, and she slowly leans forward until her cheek is touching his hand again.)

(She closes her eyes.)

SARAH. Sweet-talker.

(He laughs.)

JIM. You're not gonna faint or anything, are you? Bite off your tongue? I'm not really ready for that kind of commitment...

(She shakes her head slightly, dragging his hand across her face, and takes his fingers into her mouth.)

(long pause)

(A sound from upstairs. **SARAH** *slides away from* **JIM** *along the couch as* **MAXINE** *appears on the stairs.)*

MAXINE. Hey–

SARAH. Mom...

MAXINE. You guys okay?

SARAH. Yeah. We're not quite done yet. Cleaning. Sorry...

MAXINE. Leave it. You must be exhausted. *(beat)* Is it okay if I sit with you guys for a minute? I could use a breather.

JIM. Sure.

SARAH. Of course.

*(***SARAH*** *slides further down the couch and* **MAXINE** *sits down between them.)*

MAXINE. I thought I'd give them some time together. To reconnect.

SARAH. Good idea.

(beat)

MAXINE. So what were you guys talking about down here?

SARAH. Nothing.

MAXINE. *(teasing* **JIM***)* Not the same talk you had with Davey, I hope.

JIM. No. Poetry, mostly.

MAXINE. Oh. She's good, isn't she, Jim? Did she show you her–

JIM. Yeah. She is.

MAXINE. I used to worry, with Sidney's talent, I'd contaminate the gene pool or something.

JIM. Not a chance. You did well.

(**MAXINE** *puts her arm around* **SARAH** *and kisses her.*)

MAXINE. Yeah, she takes after him, as a writer, doesn't she? Of course, her work is very different, but–

JIM. I've only seen the one, so...

MAXINE. Take my word for it. It would have to be, I guess. Being a woman. In today's world? More vulnerable or something. "Ductile," I think Pound says–

SARAH. Less "penetrating"?

(**MAXINE** *laughs, starts to take her mask off.*)

MAXINE. Yes. Well, I don't know how to say it... Sidney's writing is really kind of macho in its way, isn't it? When we first met, I was sure he was gay. But in his writing, he has kind of– bigger balls.

JIM. *(laughs)* When was this?

MAXINE. Oh, in school. He was my TA. I was never much into writing. Kind of a sheltered childhood. Unsophisticated. More of a jock, I guess.

SARAH. That's not true.

MAXINE. It is. I ran track in high school. Used to love to jog... Even after Sarah was born. Marathons. Down to Battery Park. The Hudson River. It should be throbbing, you know, neon pink, with all the sludge they dump in there. But it's sparkling and beautiful sometimes, like a postcard... *(She shakes her head.)* At any rate, you have to train your gaze. Avoid looking at the barges, the smog, *New Jersey. (She laughs.)* I used to take the kids outside, you know, in a stroller. We didn't know much about Davey's condition then. I took them to the museums, galleries, because it was cleaner there. Air-conditioned. But even the art we saw was just– Elephant dung? I'd be covering their eyes half the time, just to get to the Baroque room.

Sidney's able to– filter these things better than I am. But Sarah takes after me that way. Sensitive to outside influence... That's why it's lucky she's here. Exposed to great art, you know. Music. Poetry. Not to all the violence, pornography, the *sewer* of pop culture we all take for granted these days. Unlike the rest of us, she had a chance to develop a healthy mind.

(**SARAH** *laughs quietly.*)

MAXINE. What? You don't think that's true?

SARAH. I don't know if you know what's in my mind, Mom...

MAXINE. Well, why don't you tell me?

SIDNEY. Max..?

(*They all look up.*)

(**SIDNEY** *has come onto the landing, leading* **DAVEY**.)

(**DAVEY** *looks like a corpse, pale and distorted. He is shirtless, clutching his oxygen mask to his face, with little red needle scars clustered around his chest.*)

(**SIDNEY** *is now showered and dressed in a simple cotton smock, like* **MAXINE**'s. *He wears a paper mask and carries a deck of cards.*)

MAXINE. Davey..? What are you..?

SIDNEY. He's feeling much better. It's all right.

(**MAXINE** *gets up and crosses to the stairs, putting on her mask as she goes.*)

MAXINE. He shouldn't be up yet. It's too soon.

SIDNEY. I tried to keep him in bed, but– He wanted to say goodbye to Jim. He insisted.

JIM. Oh, God. That's nice, Dave– But you didn't have to–

SIDNEY. I think he likes you.

SARAH. Hi, Davey.

(**DAVEY** *waves.*)

SIDNEY. Anyway, we've been having a really nice talk upstairs. I was telling him, I don't feel so great myself, tonight. A bit of an overload even for me, apparently... *Glade* is still burning in my nostrils.

MAXINE. Of course. Air "freshener" is designed to deaden your sense of smell, not *freshen* anything. Filled with formaldehyde and fatty esters. It's like taking a shot of novocaine up your nose.

SIDNEY. He was showing me some tricks too. Incredible.

JIM. Yeah, I saw.

SIDNEY. He wanted to do one more, before you go. If that's all right.

JIM. Oh. Of course. That'd be great.

(They all look at DAVEY.)

(He takes the deck of cards from SIDNEY and shuffles it expertly with one hand.)

SIDNEY. Okay, bud. Ready..? *(In the voice of a carnival barker.)* All right. Pick a card, any card–

(DAVEY holds out the deck and SIDNEY takes a card. He shows it to the rest.)

The Queen of Spades.

(He puts it back in the deck and DAVEY reshuffles. He glances at SIDNEY.)

SIDNEY. I'm supposed to say the magic word now... Um... "Talitha koum!" Right?

(DAVEY nods. He squeezes the deck, and the cards SPRAY out of his hand, fluttering down off the stair-case, all over the room.)

(MAXINE immediately starts picking them up off the floor, brushing off the oil and blood.)

MAXINE. That's okay, honey. You want to try it again..?

SIDNEY. No no no, it's– Part of the trick, Max. Ready?

(DAVEY nods)

SIDNEY. *(cont.)* Okay. Jim. Look in your wallet.

>   *(Beat. They all look at* JIM.*)*

JIM. Yeah?

>   (JIM *takes out his wallet, opens it, and draws out the Queen of Spades.)*

SIDNEY. Ta-da!

JIM. Wow. That's… incredible, Dave… Fantastic, really. How did you–

SARAH. Better make sure your money's all there.

>   (JIM *laughs.)*

JIM. Wow… I'm just–

SIDNEY. More than meets the eye, huh?

JIM. Absolutely.

MAXINE. See that, Sarah?

SARAH. Yeah, I did.

>   *(beat)*

SIDNEY. So… Jim, thanks for helping clean up, it's–

JIM. Oh, sure. Glad I could do a tiny bit. I wish I could do more.

MAXINE. Thank you though, you've been really…

SIDNEY. So, I guess I'll see you in class Monday?

JIM. Yeah.

SIDNEY. Remember, you have a sestina to write. And it better be good too. No excuses. Just because we ruined your weekend and gave you *nightmares* for the rest of your life…

>   (JIM *laughs.)*

JIM. No, it was nice. To meet you all. You've got a brilliant family here, Sid. I'm really sorry it was so–

SIDNEY. Not your fault. Stop saying you're sorry.

JIM. *(laughs)* Okay, yeah. "Multiple Apology Disorder." Runs in my family.

SIDNEY. Let me sign your thing at least, before you go…

JIM. That's all right, Sid. Some other time. *(He glances at* **SARAH**.*)* So, I'm gonna go then– All right?

(He gathers his things.)

SARAH. Dad..?

SIDNEY. Yeah, Honey?

SARAH. *(She takes a deep breath.)* Um… I was thinking I might go out with Jim tonight, if that's all right… For a drink? Just an hour or so..?

(Everybody looks at **SARAH**.*)*

MAXINE. Outside..?

SARAH. Yeah. Just for a little while… He invited me. To a reading. And I thought I might actually like to see what it's like, you know? Other writers.

JIM. Open mic. At the Union.

SIDNEY. Right. I forgot.

*(***SIDNEY*** glances at* **MAXINE**.*)*

JIM. I thought– Maybe she should see what's out there, you know. College. Student poets. Suss out the competition.

SARAH. It sounds like fun, Dad. Just a test drive. Little step. To see how I feel… So that I can decide whether or not I really–

MAXINE. Your brother almost died tonight, Sarah.

(beat)

SARAH. I know, but he's okay now, right? I mean Jim and I made a plan.

MAXINE. He needs you.

SARAH. Not really, I don't think– He seems much better. Davey? Is it okay with you if I–

MAXINE. That's not fair. To ask him. Make him feel guilty about what he can't help, honey. What he can't–

SARAH. But I–

MAXINE. Sarah, please– We can't deal with two emergencies tonight. One per day is the limit. We need you to be… For us all to get some sleep… Recharge our batteries.

SARAH. I'm not gonna have an emergency. I have my kit.
I'll be fine. And I'll call if I–

MAXINE. That's not the point. What if something happens?

SARAH. Nothing will. It's just– a poetry reading. A college
campus. I mean, what could be more painfully,
humiliatingly *safe?*

(beat)

MAXINE. You're not ready.

SARAH. How do you know?

MAXINE. I know. I've been out there. I've seen–

SARAH. I'm nineteen.

MAXINE. You can't possibly–

SARAH. I can, sure. Why not?

MAXINE. You don't know– What it's like.

SARAH. I'll find out. Mom, just because you can't leave the
house, doesn't mean I have to be–

MAXINE. I can't leave because my children / are–

SARAH. I'm not sick! *(beat, and then, calmly:)* I'm not sick,
Mom. That's you. Not me. You don't want to go out,
fine. Let Davey protect you. He's really good at it.

MAXINE. "Protect?" You think– I'm making this up? Is that
what? You think your brother– *(re:* **SIDNEY***)* He's turned
you against me, I know. But it's clear what happened
here tonight. Look– Even he can't deny it. We had
a witness. An outsider. And it was unequivocal! *(now
appealing to* **JIM***:)* You saw! Could Davey have faked
that? He stopped breathing. He almost died! He *bled.*
Out of his mouth. His nose. Is that a magic trick? Is
that a– a fucking illusion?

JIM. I'm sorry, I'm not–

MAXINE. Tell me. What you saw. You have eyes. Explain–

JIM. I'm not an expert. A doctor. A psychiatrist. / I can't–

MAXINE. Psychiatrist? *(She laughs.)* You think I'm– Uh-huh...
Okay. All of you... *(beat)* You know, they had to shut
down half of Austin last week? You read about this?

The birds were dying. People came outside, for the morning commute, and there were pigeons, sparrows, crows, littered on the highway. They had to quarantine the city, until they could decide what– What gas. What virus… And then, of course, they found nothing. Nothing! So after a few days, they opened the stores, they went about their business. They told everybody to go shopping! *(She laughs.)* Are you people blind? You have eyes? How can you not be scared?

SARAH. Dad..?

(SIDNEY looks at MAXINE.)

(long pause)

SIDNEY. I'm sorry, Honey, but… Maybe it's not the best night… To go out right now. I could really use your help. Cleaning this up, I think. We all could.

(SARAH seems to shrink into herself. She nods.)

Maybe it's better, to wait and see. Now that I know how serious– We can't risk having another reaction. Not while Davey's so… Just for a little while, okay? Until we get well again…

(SARAH looks helplessly at JIM.)

JIM. I'd better go… I'm sorry. I shouldn't have– intruded here, tonight.

MAXINE. It's not your fault.

JIM. *(nods)* Davey… It was nice meeting you, spaceman… I hope you feel better soon.

(DAVEY waves wordlessly, without taking off his mask.)

(JIM nods. He glances at SARAH, picks up his shoes, and exits, shutting the door quietly behind him.)

(long pause)

MAXINE. Sarah? Can you help your father clean up? Please? I have to bathe Davey before bed. It's been a really, really long day…

SARAH. Sure.

(beat)

MAXINE. Sidney, can you–

SIDNEY. Of course. I'm here. I'll take care of it.

(He picks up the cotton bag.)

*(**SARAH** looks around, dazed. She nods, and starts to pick things up off the coffee table.)*

MAXINE. We'll talk. About the college thing. Later. Maybe things will get better..?

*(**SARAH** nods.)*

*(**MAXINE** starts to help **DAVEY** up the stairs.)*

*(**SIDNEY** turns on the filters, which rattle for a moment, and then start to blow mist into the air.)*

*(**SARAH** cleans automatically. Picking up **SIDNEY**'s gym bag, she uncovers the paperback of Rochester's poetry.)*

SARAH. *(almost to herself, wondering)* Hey– He forgot his book… *(She picks up the book, looks at the cover.)* Dad, look, the book you lent him…

SIDNEY. It's okay. Put it in the bookshelf. He'll find another copy.

*(**SARAH** leafs through the pages.)*

SARAH. I could bring it to him… You know, I could–

SIDNEY. That's all right. I'll / take care of it.

SARAH. He might need it tonight though. To study. For his writing.

MAXINE. Sidney can give it to him in class tomorrow.

SARAH. It's Friday, Mom… He'll need it this weekend.

MAXINE. If he really needs it, he can go to the library. He's not a child.

SARAH. But I can still catch him on the street, if I hurry–

MAXINE. Sarah, don't be ridiculous. It's the middle of the night. You're not even dressed properly…

SARAH. I can still catch him. Outside–

(She grabs a pair of white sneakers and pulls them onto her feet.)

MAXINE. Sid–

(SIDNEY doesn't move.)

(MAXINE comes stumbling down the stairs, trying to push past him, to get to SARAH.)

(DAVEY makes a loud rasping noise underneath his mask. He almost falls off the stairs, clutching the banister to keep himself upright.)

(MAXINE hesitates, torn between going after SARAH and helping DAVEY.)

MAXINE. Wait– Listen– You don't know what it's like out there, honey. What it's–

(DAVEY makes another sound and MAXINE staggers back up the stairs.)

MAXINE. Please. Look– Listen to me!

(SARAH looks back at them, standing on the stairs, DAVEY leaning on MAXINE's arm.)

(She waves once, simply, and exits, slamming the front door.)

(SIDNEY, MAXINE, and DAVEY stand there together, silently, breathing through their masks.)

(The hum of the air filters.)

(Lights fade.)

END OF PLAY.

ACKNOWLEDGEMENTS

SICK was written with inspiration and input from many writers, directors, actors, and friends. I finished the first draft in Marsha Norman's workshop at NYU, and I must be the ten thousandth former student to thank her for her keen eye, brilliant mind, and passionate advocacy of new plays and playwrights. Mark Dickerman, Greg Keller, Dave Auburn, Vivienne Benesch, Aimée Hayes, Thai Jones, Harry Kellerman, Tom Meredith, Bear Korngold, Logan Lavail, Edith Freni, Colin McKenna, Molly Smith Metzler, Kenneth DeWoskin, Kathy Boudin, Chesa Boudin, and Malik Dohrn all offered critical feedback and solidarity. And Judith DeWoskin, in addition to being a wonderful reader, lovingly gave me the time to write.

Chris Carlos, Tina Parker, and the creative team at Kitchen Dog pulled Sick from their slush pile and gave it the kind of scorching world premiere every playwright imagines, at the kind of bold, risk-taking company the American theatre so desperately needs.

Many other theaters contributed to the play's development. The Alliance, Magic Theatre, MCC, The Public, and Aurora Theatre did early readings, and productions at the Chautauqua Institute, New Jersey Rep, Southern Rep, and the Berkshire Theatre Festival helped inform later drafts.

Phyllis Wender supported this play, as she does all my work, with ferocity, integrity, wit, and warmth. I am grateful to have her in my corner.

Bill Ayers and Bernardine Dohrn, both committed citizens and public intellectuals, gave me a model for living and writing in the world.

And Rachel DeWoskin is the genius in all my work – love is not a prison, and there is someone for everyone, turns out.

Also by

Zayd Dohrn...

Outside People

Reborning